FABIANA ELISA MARTÍNEZ

CONQUERED BY FOG

Short stories

Pierre Turcotte Editor

© 2023 Pierre Turcotte Éditeur. Tous droits réservés.
Dépôt légal – Bibliothèque et Archives nationales du Québec,
Bibliothèque et Archives Canada, 2023.
ISBN : 978-2-925219-80-4

CONQUERED BY FOG

To Quin Mathews, my friend.

Prologue by Raúl Lavalle

According to the Fathers of the Church, "a teacher is a father to his students." I always say that my students are my children. Since Fabiana Martínez was my student several decades ago in faraway Buenos Aires (an excellent disciple of ancient Greek and Latin), I dare to say that *Conquered by Fog* is my progeny.

I believe that her other professors and I contributed to Fabiana's first steps toward a sober and careful narrative style, cultured without overwhelming erudition, refined without pedantry, and frankly enjoyable. Perhaps she possesses the correctness of those who take great care in a second language: they are more English than the English, almost obsessive about being correct, like Eliza Doolittle in *Pygmalion*. (Another character thought she was from some Eastern European country because she was so precise in expressing herself in the language of Daniel Defoe).

What I have just said is well confirmed in "Predictions," a story set in Rome that combines tender and measured love and many references to Italian, etymologies, and the traditions of the Eternal City.

But "Predictions" is not the only nostalgic story in this collection. "Truth" is based on the keeping of a boy's memory of the aerial and ghostly beauty of a stewardess named Diana, a name he liked "for that was Ben's favorite Roman deity" (again, recurring mythology).

"Hidden Places" is not so much about real places (like those rare corners of cities, which we curious tourists love so much), but about a *locus mentis*, about places "of our souls," as Fabiana says. And sometimes the arrival of a person, especially a young one, to a paralyzed and dark world becomes "a ray of sun." It reminds me of the young girl's appearance at a gloomy home in Salem in *The House of the Seven Gables*. "Hidden Places" does not lack an unexpected ending, which I leave to your reading.

"Risks" is a beautiful story of love between children depicting the apprehension that a tender first-person narrator feels before conversing with an extremely well-read little girl who likes to take refuge in a rarely visited corner of a religious school. I disagree with the narrator who claims that the kiss they gave each other was "the stupidest first kiss in history and I've ruined this page in our biography forever." Writers sometimes lie (maybe it's the only thing we do), and here I think he's fooling us too, for the first kiss is always remembered. Delicious story, sealed with a kiss!

As for "Conquered by Fog," the story that gives its name to the book, it brings to an everyday situation—the blindness of a dog—Platonic philosophy, in particular the famous allegory of the cave. There is more than one lesson in this text, but I mention this one: We may be blind or lack some natural gift, but there exists in all orders of life (in entertainment, in economics, in law, in linguistics) a wise law of compensation. The virtue of prudence teaches us to live with what we do not have.

I have briefly mentioned some of the stories in this collection. I liked all of them very much, and I recommend them to you, sweet reader, sure that I am not mistaken. Fabiana extracts universal value from everyday situations. She is aided by her great culture, her taste for travel, her resistance to paying excessive tribute to the charms of fashion, her careful prose—which knows that a great book can be a great evil—, not just a little English humor, and knowing how to appreciate the good things in the lives we live today.

Professor Raúl Lavalle
Latin and Ancient Greek Professor
Universidad Católica Argentina

Thief

Over the course of the four decades of her life, Marina stole three distinctive things and never fathomed the shameful idea that any of them would have to be returned.

Her first act of thievery occurred when she was five years old and for an almost experimental purpose. The object was a random blue piece that belonged to an assembling game that she used to love in kindergarten. Sister Amélie was always very adamant about how good girls kept their classroom in order and never, ever, took any toys or staples home. Stealing was a sin. God was constantly watching and our obligation consisted in taking care of all the beautiful gifts our Eternal Father provided for us. In mid-year, Marina was so bored by the same comminatory speech, decanted every afternoon before school was over, that she slipped the useless plastic square in her pocket. She wanted to prove to herself that her growing assumption was accurate: how could they know she had done it? Thus, the worn-out piece remained in her undiscovered possession for many years cornered in the bottom of a drawer by other dead mementos of childhood and corroborating to its illicit owner that, like the tree falling in the forest, a sin needs a witness more tangible than God to exist.

The second appropriation had taken place when Marina was twenty-three, two days after she had broken up with the shy boy she had called her boyfriend for the last six years. Marina had gone to his apartment, the new one he wanted to use to explore more adventurous attractions to which Marina had not been offered a ticket. There were not many things to recover from the place she would not visit again but, while looking at the bookshelves, Marina saw the thin red book she had caressed dearly many times. While touching the cloth covers again with the tip of her fingers, as if touching the ears of a stray cat rubbing against her knees, Marina remembered the improper but wise theory of Professor Devedia. People only steal two things without feeling guilty: books and other people's spouses. The reason, the sturdy matron of Aesthetics II used to say, was that the thieves buried their crime under the benign belief that books and spouses can be licitly stolen when they are not well taken care of by their authorized owners. Marina smiled and with the same excitement of her first childhood offense, stole *Le Nouveau Bescherelle 1, L'Art de Conjuguer* and promised herself to master the language of Balzac.

When she committed her third infraction, her state of fear, pain and ecstatic infatuation was such that she could not remember that, in order to help the owner of the picture, she had reviewed the rules of his language with the added pleasure of practicing verb conjugations from a stolen red-covered book.

Nicolas had materialized in her academic path as a predictable nuisance and in her love life as a knight-rescuer of broken hopes worthy of the troops of Charlemagne. Professor Devedia had informed her that as part of her doctorate program, she would have to help Professor Nicolas Lalanne in his three-month research about the influence of Andre Breton in the works of two contemporary Peruvian writers. Marina was the only one of the fellows who would be able to comprehend Monsieur Lalanne's words and destroy that same language clumsily trying to make herself understood. Marina accepted the responsibility with stoicism, like someone who knows that a heavy, beautifully wrapped present is just a dusty brick with no value. Babysitting a snobby, round-glasses, young French of her *professeur* was not her ideal plan for the winter of her twenty-seventh birthday. But when Monsieur Lalanne opened the door of the study hall and let her in, Marina noticed he did not wear any glasses and that with some invisible prestidigitation, this man had thrown the imaginary brick straight at her chest and shattered the wall of ice that many disrupted love affairs had helped to build inside her.

For two months work took them to libraries and museums, cafes and train stations, the houses of lost writers who offered them bread and whiskey and, finally, three weeks before his grant was over, to his bed, *un lit* for a love made in fragments of languages they did not share completely but managed to arrange in a Frankenstein-styled dismembered lexicon that their bodies did not need to obey the international laws of desire.

On the evening of Marina's birthday, while she was trying to wake in the lake of his sheets and decipher what was the best term to define this new intoxicating feeling, Nicolas came back from the kitchen with a glass of wine, sat on her side of the bed, caressed her forehead, and with an accent that melted any remains of forgotten sorrows, said: "*Ma belle*, I am leaving tomorrow."

Marina looked at him from the placid haze of untold love, barely heard some words about a family emergency, about responsibilities far away, about her being the only reason why he had stayed this long, and let him go back to check on his special ratatouille with which they would celebrate and also say their sad good-byes. She knew at that moment that her time was limited and let her eyes wander to find where her clothes were and which souvenir she would take without guilt, without a witness. She grabbed one of the two pictures lying on the nightstand, the one of Nicolas and the other handsome man leaning against a veranda by a faraway river in the south of France. Marina did not know who the freckled girl on the remaining picture was and did not have the time or the will to inquire. She hid the chosen picture inside the book she carried in her purse, walked through the dark hallway to her private French cook and kissed him in the neck to make sure that her new crime would be enveloped forever in his unforgettable smell.

Marina's own river of youth continued flowing slowly and unstoppably after Nicolas left. Professor Devedia died in the most inelegant way during a class about the Apollonian concept of beauty. Marina took her place, married and divorced a man she never completely loved, lost an undesired pregnancy and waded through the swirl of days while teaching Aesthetics. The older she grew, the more she understood the second inconvenient theory of Professor Devedia. Beauty is not perceived because of its perfection, nor because of its intrinsic goodness or its undeniable truth.

Beauty is what remains beyond imperfection, what shines through the claws of mud and pain. The Venus de Milo is flawless because she lacks her arms. We are free to imagine them as we please, we could offer her ours if we wanted. What the hand of man or the breeze of time takes away from these pieces is what makes them more beautiful than they would be if they were complete.

The night of Marina's fortieth birthday, she got an e-mail in the university mailbox from an unknown sender. The subject line, perfectly written in her language, said: I would love to see you again. The lines that followed were all in French, a language that Marina had finally mastered with the help of two ideal tools: a scarred heart and a stolen book.

Two days before knocking on his hotel room, Marina tried to find a modern picture of Nicolas. Nowadays there is no need to steal physical pictures anymore, everything is exposed, available, obscenely out until the end of time to satiate the hunger of multiple robbers. Either she could not find any images of him linked to his name or she decided not to look anymore after she recognized the face of the other man as young and handsome as in the picture inside her book. And she learned the scorching truth that Christian Lalanne had died thirteen years ago after the cruel caress of unjust fate had touched his noble heart. Christian's parents, his beautiful freckled daughter and his brother Nicolas had been at his side during the few agonizing weeks.

"*Ma belle ! Chérie !*" said *Professeur* Lalanne still not leaning to kiss her. Marina smiled. She had found the secret of permanent youth. Even with his blue squared glasses and his added wrinkles, she saw him with her distorting younger eyes and was convinced that he was experiencing the same.

"*Ça va ?*" Marina asked before their ageless embrace, a hug she could only do with one arm while securing with the other a book that hid the image of a graceful man who had been taken away too early, a returned lover who had come at last, and the confession of a girl who had stolen just three things in her life and was ready to return the most important one of them.

Predictions

« Aeneas, servant of the gods, ascends
The templed hill where lofty Phoebus reigns,
And that far-off, inviolable shrine
Of dread Sibylla, in stupendous cave,
O'er whose deep soul the god of Delos breathes
Prophetic gifts, unfolding things to come. »

P. Vergilius Maro, *Aeneid*, Book VI, 9-12

By the time the plane landed in Fiumicino, all the people at home who knew about my trip were placing bets, including my wife. They knew that in a couple of days I would be under the sheets with the great Giulia Magaldi. The bets did not debate if the affair would exist but how long the obvious miracle would take to ignite.

Silvia came out of the plane first and set foot on her former land with too much strength for having flown for more than nine hours. She knew the airport better. In fact, for the last couple of years since the day she came to assist me on this delirious project, I had learned to accept the undeniable truth that Silvia tended to know everything much better than any other member of the crew. It was not only about checking the language of half of the script or the accuracy of the Roman settings, nor was it because of the discussions she helped me endure with the Italian producers or with Giulia Magaldi's agent. It was almost the fleeting certainty that she knew the language she taught and shared but also the feelings that propelled those words, the images that invoked those feelings, the bodies of art from which those images sprouted. At the luggage claim area, tiredly patient, Silvia waited for me to gather all the equipment, the tripod and the boom, and then walked out to grab a taxi that appeared to be waiting just for her since the time she had left her city in order to pursue her Californian dream.

"Andiamo a Lungotevere Arnaldo da Brescia due, per favore!" she ordered the driver in the slightly higher volume that always accompanied her mother tongue.

"I know what that word means, *lungotevere*," I said with the three-year-old pride I tend to offer her when I know a word that she has not taught me yet.

"Do you?" she questioned with a benevolent smile, one of those tender smirks she saves for me when I don't know a word I assume I know.

"It means 'I will see you soon'. *Lungo-te-vere*." But before finishing the sentence I knew I was infinitely wrong and I didn't care. She would be gentle, she would caress my broken ego generously with a new explanation and would restore my shattered self-esteem with the balm of her sparkling piece of knowledge.

"No, *signore direttore*, it doesn't mean that. I like your inventive lexiconic try, though. It means literally 'a path along the Tiber'. That is where our hotel is. Remember? That was one of Giulia's contractual requests: *Signora* Magaldi can only be calm and rehearse properly by looking at the river of her childhood. Oh God, what a brat! Keep my words, Abbott, you may be the star director of this movie who falls in love with every gorgeous promise of the screen, but this woman will break your heart and dry the vaults in the banks of your producers."

Silvia always said "keep my words" instead of "mark my words". I had never had the courage to correct her. Perhaps because she was a linguistic authority for me and also because I liked to keep her words, every new phonetic treasure she shared with me. Words are the presents you can give and still preserve with you, she also said. And, as always, she was right.

She thanked the taxi driver, ran through the majestic doors and, by the time all my luggage was in the lobby, she had checked us in. I could understand every single word the stiff concierge was saying, but I preferred to let her lead the conversation. She had told me once that whoever decides to learn a new language, no matter how old he is, becomes a toddler again. She was right. It took me a while to surrender my power. I am used to controlling people, I am a director. But my mastery embraces colors and frames, special organizations of scenery and actors. The words I direct have been previously written, rehearsed, listened and forcibly forgotten by actors whenever a scene has to be repeated. Around Silvia, on the contrary, words don't follow a choreography; the new language directs the director.

"Do you like the arrangements?" Silvia asked, taking me away from my daydream, from the lobby of this ancient palazzo, from the De Chirico on a distant wall. "Giulia has already arrived. Her room is on the second floor, her assistant's and mine are on the third. And you are on the fourth, the whole attic is yours. Here is your key, *la sua chiave signore direttore*."

I was happy. The arrangement was indeed perfect. Silvia would never be sure about my escapades to the second floor, to sensual Giulia. Hopefully most nights of this adventurous trip to check locations and do private rehearsals with the great Giulia Magaldi, Silvia would see me candidly go with her in the elevator to my attic without a hint of lust in my eyes. Silvia would still respect me. Not like all the others at home betting on my lecherous directing ways with voluptuous actresses and on *Signora* Magaldi's passionate manners with every single director she acts for.

The morning of the third day, a Friday, our actress had a perfunctory headache that pushed Silvia and me in the direction of Piazza del Popolo in search of a *farmacia*. The Italian assistant was too busy holding

Giulia's heavily ringed hand to abate the migraine. When we left the Palazzo, I knew that the diva's ailment was a coded message for me, a way to play guilty for the kiss she had secretly stolen from me the previous night over too many martinis, her showing her decision of opening her room to me that very night. What a weekend I had in front of me!

The river was grayish green that morning and a small flock of crows flew away in the direction of Ponte Margherita the moment we came out of the building.

"Hmmm, they flew to the left," Silvia said with sadness. "Bad augury."

"What are you saying? Bad birthday? Isn't *auguri* birthday in Italian, or wishes, or something they sing at birthday parties?"

"Abbot, I am speaking English. Augury, omen," she sentenced.

I did not ask what she meant. It did not make sense. I learned in all these years of dealing with young, interesting women that I should not ask when something seems too obvious for them and too complicated for me. We needed a pharmacy, not an etymology class.

We rehearsed some lines in the afternoon. Giulia had to learn a dialogue in English. Silvia repeated the scene with her thirty-one times. I just wanted the evening to throw its silent cape over us soon, I wanted to be opening the door on the second floor that the green eyes of Giulia were inviting me to push every time she looked up in search of my acceptance, while Silvia tried to make clear for her the pronunciation of the character's words.

The night finally walked in. Giulia excused herself from our table at the terrace too early. She was cautious to send me a last green look of welcoming approval. The assistant followed her with a weary pace. Silvia and I breathed the Roman sky for some minutes, without a sound. I was ready to leave and make happy all those idiots who had bet that I would embrace Giulia Magaldi no later than our third night in the city of Venus.

The concierge stopped Silvia before we got in the elevator. I was too anxious to follow his apologetic words. I did not care about the end of the world as long as it was some hours ahead of us. Silvia walked back pensively and pushed the button to the third floor without looking at me.

"What did he say?" I asked.

"The elevator is not going to the fourth. You need to take the stairs from the third floor to get to the attic. Some kind of… *problema tecnico*."

We got out at her floor and we stood in the minuscule rounded landing. She had her key in her hand and was fidgeting with it when she looked up at me.

"*Buona notte*, Abbott. Have nice dreams."

The sound of her words was echoing the wings of the morning birds. Her bright eyes were allowing me to be the translator just for once. And they said more than I wanted to know. I was in the land of Aeneas, in front of my Sibyl, my Silvia, the beautiful prophetess who would not lead me to the lower world but would show me who I really loved. I knew that it was with her and with her voice and next to her adamant energy I wanted to sleep that night. But her eyes and her hesitant key were telling me that the risk was too high, our complicity too deep and we both would lose forever the tempting feeling of never knowing how our secret love could be. "*Buona notte, bella signorina*," I said a second too late. And we both knew at that moment that I would never sleep with her but I would always have her at my side.

By the time I got to my solitary attic, I had forgotten Giulia Magaldi within a sumptuous, bottomless yawn.

Truth

The very first time that a real woman touched Ben, he was fourteen, confused and distracted. The second time, he was alert.

Surely other women had caressed, held, and even hit him in the course of his brief life. But all those ladies had had a higher title to carry in the script of his days. All of them, mother, aunts, nannies, teachers, and grandmothers (although Ben could not find the image of his paternal grandmother extending her hands to anybody) were like planets in a system and each of them had performed their steps according to a strict choreography in the ballroom of Ben's development. All of those women had been and still were essential elements of the algorithm that coded Ben's activities. Some nurtured, others corrected, most of them protected and a few signaled the path. Their touches and voices, their eyes and skins could be young, decrepit, intense, or reticent. Certainly, none of their acts were deprived of sense.

But Diana, he hoped the name on her Pan Am nametag was her real name for that was Ben's favorite Roman deity, was nothing more than a woman who had touched him twice. Years later, whenever he breathed the nauseating scent of mothballs, usually when Jennifer took him to see a classic play at the Lyric Stage on Clarendon Street on a Sunday afternoon, he wondered if that odor had brought Diana to his rescue. He was covering his mouth with one hand and rummaging in the front seat pocket in search of the sanitary bag that might prevent an accident in the hours to come. The flight was packed and he was not sure if he would be able to endure the emanations from the pink Chanel jacket to his right for the entire four hours from Love Field to Logan.

"Let me check your seat belt, honey," a voice sang while the most immaculate red nails crowning the fingers of an exquisite hand interrupted his quest. Ben looked up, forgot that he was part of a universe in which fat ladies in stinking outfits sat in planes next to teenagers who traveled alone, and let Diana shake the buckle while smiling at him and frowning her nose. As her pinky finger slightly brushed against his shirt, Ben sat still, appalled by the effort of understanding the tide of shame and pleasure that rose to his face faster than any Apollo mission so far.

As the plane took off, Ben's bafflement sparkled with the new happiness of understanding that four hours would not be enough to process the feeling. He smiled at his cartoon magazine because the panels depicting Yuri Gagarin's life would become the innocent parapet from which to follow the steps of Diana up and down the aisle. When the creamy clown inside the Chanel jacket began to snore, Ben reclined his seat and pretended to read while praying to all the ancient Roman pantheon that the next blue skirt rubbing his shoulder belonged to the blond reincarnation of its hunting goddess.

But gods retire in more drastic ways than humans do, or they tend to become deaf even before retiring. Diana was not the one bringing him the mid-flight bitter orange juice and crackers, nor the one clicking her blue shoes to the front of the cabin to describe the weather conditions at landing, nor the one collecting the trash.

Gagarin was about to start his last flight in his MIG-15 in the third panel of page 58 when the living pilot announced that their descent had begun. In a string of movements hard to enumerate, the pink jacket stopped snoring, Ben closed his magazine, and a hand touched his hair.

"Please straighten your seat, sir," Diana said. Ben looked into her eyes and turned into the smallest being on Earth, smaller than any Earthling Gagarin could have fathomed from space. Each stroke of the red nails on his hair made him even more diminutive pushing him irremediably to the verge of disappearance. "You have the softest hair I've ever touched, darling. Thank you for flying with us."

Years passed and over their relentless trail of seconds Ben did not have to visit uncle Kevin in Texas anymore, Pan Am went bankrupt, and the number of Chanel suits on planes decreased immensely. At least for Ben, the truth remained, however, in the atoms of what really mattered: the smell of mothballs, the bitterness of cheap orange juice, and the first brush of sensuality dropped like a present from an ancient, flying nymph.

Stupidity

"You may jeer at our stupidity and at our inexperience in business matters; you have done all you could already to make us look ridiculous; but do not dare to call us dishonest."

Fyodor Dostoyevsky, *The Idiot*

The name of the church added one more irony to the list. That not all trinities are holy was the second thought that Alejandra's mind created while she lowered her eyes from the vaulted ceiling, trying to protect them from the obscene glowing of the stained- glass. She did not mean to be sacrilegious, only accurate. Her breath was calmer now after the steep run to reach the atrium and the preliminary confusion at finding the correct pew. She was never late but, curiously, this time she had arrived two minutes after the organ yawned its solemn notes and when the pastor was greeting the attendants. The first thought Alejandra had was the sacrilegious one: Audrey looked hyperbolically old, tired and defeated.

The solemn usher had shown her the vacant space on the fifth pew to the left. There was one space close to the aisle. Understandably, the couple sitting next to her did not want to interact too much with the aisle pilgrims or the direct family sitting in the center section. Because of their distant respect for the mourners, Alejandra ended up sitting five rows behind Audrey, who was at the very front, hugged by her son and supervised by her daughter-in-law. Alejandra realized that this one would be her last and longest opportunity to look at Audrey at ease in real life with the same impunity that she had been watching her anonymously in tens of pictures irresponsibly scattered by the winds of cyberspace.

The church was orderly full with mourners, all straight and seated, black pieces of candy in a semicircular tin made of wood and glass. Nobody had to stand in the back or in the upper balcony with the scrawny organist. It was, therefore, a properly filled-up church, a cleanly attended funeral, the right balance of emotionless sorrow and evenness, as proper and slick as Alejandra knew Audrey loved things. The last time Alejandra had seen the family together had been also in a church, forty-five years ago and many thousand miles away. Audrey was leading her exquisite family to present their respects to Mary, Joseph, and the baby in the manger. The three of them had been chosen as the exemplary family in the expat community to take the responsibilities of the three wise men nobody wanted to impersonate. Alejandra was sitting much farther from them that Christmas day than today, but still remembered Audrey's quiet reverence, her young son's exuded nervousness, and her husband's badly hidden anxiety. Churches seemed to bring the four of them together, Alejandra smiled to herself, either for the birth of Jesus or the death of Harry.

It was a deep disappointment that this church was made of glass, plaster and wood. Older churches made of stones or bricks give the saintly bored the chance to count them unaccountably until the pastor or the eulogist finishes their remarks. Alejandra could not find anything to count, and her eyes kept going back to the coffin. The gardenias on top were Audrey's favorite; Harry would have preferred lilies.

Once the pastor finished his welcoming greeting and the neat depiction of the ceremonial steps that would follow, the crew cut, square-hip dame of the church approached the microphone to guide the community through the first hymn. Alejandra did not know any religious songs in any language, she did not know how to find them in any of the sturdy books in front of her, so she stood up, regal on her high heels, maybe too high for a seventy-year-old lady, and dove in the contemplation of the main singer. Every church has one of these, she thought, a square woman who takes the earthly matters over her robust shoulders so the pastor or the priests or even a reform rabbi can attend to the incorporeal dilemmas of humans and gods. In a mischievous way, it was even delightful to look at this impartial queen of nothing and show her how she was so irreverently not singing along. Maybe it was because of Alejandra's rebellion that the churchy matron almost knocked the microphone down with one swish of her arm while drawing in the air the rhythm of the vehement verse. Harry would have laughed at the whole picture; Audrey surely frowned.

The pastor took possession of the dais again and made an invitation that everybody received with a smile, and Alejandra did not have time to dread: "Let's take some minutes to tell the person sitting next to us how we are related to the family, how we got to know

Harry and Audrey, why we love them so much." A terrified Alejandra looked down at her bony hands, crossed by deltas of bulging veins, crowned by perfect red nails and beautified by two antique rings: the one that her husband had given her two days before dying and the smaller one Harry had bestowed upon her on his last, devastating, good-bye-forever visit, twenty-five years ago. Rings are like the many men in a smart woman's heart. They can be multiple, they do not need to touch each other, and they can enhance the value of the surrounding ones. A ruby is not a diamond, an emerald is not a sapphire, and all together make her hands and her soul more alive and inscrutable.

Alejandra turned her proud head toward the couple to her left, almost with irritation. The woman was eager to tell her how she had met the family. Apparently, they did not know a lot of people at the funeral and were planning on confederating with the older lady who had arrived two minutes late to face the awkwardness of the coming tea and cookies served by the widow in the adjacent basketball court.

"Hi, I am Kathy Saunier and this is my husband, Rick. We met Audrey five years ago, when we moved here. She has been so nice to us. She is so loved at the church, so hard-working. She only wants to help people. I don't know how she found the time to do all she did and to take care of a husband with such an unjust and cruel disease for ten years! Our grandchildren called her their third grandmother! How do you know them?"

Alejandra did not know anything about Harry being sick for so long. What kind of malady was this woman trying not to mention? He had vanished from the social world, the boards over which he presided, the galas he and Audrey attended regularly. Alejandra knew he had been alive only because she had searched unsuccessfully every day for his obituary on-line for the last five years, after her own husband died, and she allowed herself the quirky behavior, taking it as a sign of old age and withered romance. The best way to lie convincingly, she knew, was to respond with a mutilated version of the truth.

"I met them many years ago, in Chile. I used to work with Harry. My name is Alejandra Ruiz."

The woman stared at her for five whole seconds that should have been two. Apparently, her open mouth could not find the right words to answer a question that Alejandra had not asked. The sounds of the pastor over the microphone came to Kathy's rescue, and Alejandra sighed. Wrinkles and a dewlap make a very effective costume. Even if people are slightly younger than you are, they tend not to believe that you could have been a young passionate lover or even a mistress.

Alejandra prepared herself for the next step. But not enough. The video to celebrate Harry's long life was so polluted with perfection and fake poses that even Audrey put down her head after some slides. And Alejandra witnessed again, possibly for the last time, how in every single picture of the happy family, it was Harry, without exception, the one trying to touch Audrey's shoulder, and how stiff

Audrey looked next to him, almost disgusted by the intended impossible caress. For such a video, Alejandra knew, Harry would have chosen a caustic Lyle Lovett song, not the melancholic Meditation from Thais or the playful flute of a Hikari Ōe's waltz to varnish the last scenes.

The pastor returned, all teary, and started his starry eulogy, stepping deeper and deeper in every new compliment to such a noble man as Harry had been. Alejandra concurred but did not understand the comment about Harry's last years' prominent imagination and his passion for characters that, of course, he had created in his mind and was happy to share with his beloved ones until the sad final silence. Characters? She could not ask anybody about them. One more secret that he had had and surely Audrey had guessed, like all his secrets.

The final hymn started, and Alejandra hurried to leave before anybody else. Unfortunately, her will was one step behind the military discipline of the square matron who intercepted her and said with a dagger-like voice: "The widow and the close family first, Madam."

Alejandra quietly cursed the woman while her eyes filled up with tears of impotence and rage that she had not born in decades. Through those tears, she saw Audrey coming down the aisle, looking at her in disbelief and terror. One tear had reached Alejandra's chin when Audrey passed by her, shielding her own chest with a tremulous hand.

After the family procession, everybody else walked slowly to the basketball court. Tea and cookies continue alluring the living, no matter how funereal they might feel. Only Alejandra walked to the ladies' room, found the farthest stall and sat inside to wait until she could stop crying and escape with dignity.

Her stupor was interrupted by two voices, one of which she recognized.

"She is real! I tell you. I talked to her! It cannot be a coincidence."

"What do you mean? That is absurd. Everybody knew he was delirious."

"Really? So, he goes for ten years in a dementia blurt, talking about and calling for this Alejandra every single day, crying for her, informing everybody every other minute that she is the love of his life, and asking if anybody has seen her lately, begging Audrey to find her and bring her to him, and then at his very funeral a random Alejandra shows up out of nowhere, and you don't believe she is real? The whole story he was telling was real!!! Don't you see, Fanny?"

Alejandra, sitting on the toilet, talked silently to her cheaper ring. "Oh, Harry, how could you be so fucking stupid." She rearranged her skirt, got out, washed her delicate hands in front of the horrified women and left the church, Audrey, and Harry's corpse to rot for eternity.

Kicks

He did not want her to move or to say anything although he knew she would, sooner rather than later. The light from a single lamp in the foreign room was made of copper and yellow tourmaline. The flashes of the faraway highway could not disturb them so high in the building.

He would have preferred that her head were a little closer to his chest, but in the haze of this most desired peace, he realized that lately, after love, she always nested her head on the oblique scar on his abdomen. He had a suspicion: she did it more as a choreographic gesture than as a sign of languor. She did it so he could not get up as easily to straighten things up right away. He caressed her hair with the tip of his fingers, the little turmoil of hazelnut and gold curls that crowned her and she would never see from his perspective. It soothed him to touch her hair without having to read the message in her eyes. He knew she was not asleep but did not want to disturb their shared cocoon of feathery silence. Would this one be at last their last time together? How could he know? He was immensely happy to have been able to perform respectably one more time, but at his age that could not be the case in the very near future. His contorted love for her would not be enough of an excuse when his physical powers decline. Better to disappear from her life in the heights of victory. He surely would miss a moment like this one, but he had a myriad of reflections of this second in his mind to drown himself in memories.

She kissed his rough skin, almost blew on his wide stomach, covered with impossibly blond hairs that were difficult to see from even that close.

"How did you get that scar?" she finally asked.

"You know", he said, elevating his head just enough to try to catch her eye without succeeding. "It's from when I had appendicitis when I was … twenty-four. Wow! Like thirty years ago! I told you the story a million times. When I was handsome, my hair was not gray, and you were a little girl," he smiled, knowing exactly how she was going to react.

"I was not a little girl, I had men falling in love around me like snowflakes in the wind! You always think I did not exist until you showed up! You still believe that's the case even now! I have a life when you disappear, you know? You really think you are the center of the universe." She fused the last sounds with another kiss on his surgical scar.

"Because I am. Of your universe at least. Am I not?"

She raised her head and wiped some strands of hair from her eyes to look at him. He knew that look of hers. Drunk and sleepy from their tumultuous demonstrations just minutes ago. One more time he was struck by her primordial image. The miracle she had been when she was twenty-three. This type of love, this lasting intrinsic knowledge they had of each other, was the only effective elixir for old age. Every time he visited her, he rationally knew he would find new wrinkles under her eyes and that the color of her hair would not be completely natural anymore. His hands could feel that her asymmetric, delightful breasts were affected now by some cruel law of merciless gravity. And even knowing all that, when she turned in such an abrupt manner and looked at him, he could only see her as she was when both had become irremediable lovers, almost as many years in the past as was her age when they met.

"I don't mean this scar. I know this one by heart. I mean the other one, on your big toe. I've never seen it before. How could there be anything on your body I've never seen before?"

He felt again the wave of urgency to tidy up the bed, the whole room. He had to get up and clean the mess they had produced, clean the traces of love from her skin at least. He was a little mad at her for playing this game of not letting him get up. How a lady so elegant and neat, so sophisticated as she had become, could turn into the carefree vixen she was on his bed, on all the uncountable beds they had shared as lover and mistress. His touch induced the magic pass by which she did not care anymore about her expensive shoes, the mix of jewelry that different men had given her over all these years, the stained sheets or her dewy breasts.

"Let me get up. I have to clean this chaos."

"No, you don't. You need to answer me first. Why do you care so much about any mess? Relax! Someone will clean it up tomorrow. That is part of the service, isn't it? You pay for it with your golden card. Tell me. How did you get that scar?"

He leaned his head back on the silk pillow that smelled like brown sugar and kept a hint of her delirious scent. He sighed. He knew he had to answer so he could get up finally and grab the airy towel he had placed strategically on a chair before he brought her up to his room, after their ceremonial dinner at the hotel bistro.

"I cut myself with a mirror." He pronounced with a raspy voice.

"Oh my! Poor thing! How did that happen? How did it break? Did it fall on your foot?"

He did not want to talk about that. A greasy guilt was about to strangle him. He only wanted to smell her, to caress her hair, the back of her neck, and the impossible softness of the valley in between her shoulders as he had done sporadically for the last twenty-three years —as he might be doing for their last time.

"I don't remember well. I was six years old."

"So, you do remember. You know you remember. You cannot lie to me. Tell me so I can cure you."

Why did she have to say those words? He did not need to be cured. He was not weak. Whenever she said words like those, he panicked and knew the time to run away from her had come. She was like this hypnotic fire that invited him to get closer and threatened to burn him alive if he did not watch his distance.

"I hit a mirror one evening I was mad."

"Mad at what?" she inquired, putting her right hand over his chest.

"I was disrespectful to a guest of my father during dinner. He was a very important man, a colleague of dad, a genius in his field. They were talking about fairy tales. I interrupted them and said those silly stories were for girls and they were stupid."

"Well, you were participating in their conversation, you were a brave boy! I bet the man laughed. Was he a writer?" She was raking his chest with her nails, gingerly, faintly. Her chin was close to his belly button. Her eyes were curious and her makeup gone.

"He didn't. My father sent me to my room. I threw the awful heavy shoes they made me wear for this special event in the air. I cried. When Mom arrived, I had broken the mirror behind the door with one kick. Mom wrapped my toe in her immaculate napkin and went back to the table, the disgusting psychologist and Dad." He put an arm over his face. He had told a very old story for the first time. He had to sleep. She had to go.

"Will I see you soon?" She asked unnecessarily, yearning for a lie. Some seconds passed without a sound. She moved to the opposite side of the bed to kiss his toe.

"I may come back next month. You know how it is." She left the room ten minutes later but not alone.

She carried on her lips the sorrows of a young boy who did not like fairy tales. The boy she has been healing for half of her life. She also cradled in her, without knowing it, another little secret made of surprise, brown sugar, and tourmaline light, who would start kicking inside her not-so-young womb sixteen weeks from this night.

Hidden Places

The first tear fell on the countertop, the second on the dog's head. Samuel put the knife down, took a deep breath, and looked at the ceiling trying to restrain the spasm of sorrow that was dashing through his chest. The dog made an almost inaudible whimpering sound. Was it checking if he was all right? Samuel had stumbled upon the lanky mutt five years ago, more bone than flesh, more mange than fur. Since the unexpected adoption, he had always wondered who had taken possession of whom. In moments like this, when tears were wasted and cooking interrupted, was when Samuel marveled about the impenetrable mind-reading skills of the dog.

It had been because of this animal, because of its scrawny figure and its need for care and special food, that Samuel had met the woman of his life, or his life in the eyes of a woman. He couldn't know that hazy morning that Diana would appropriate that role. He had not had much time to look at her. She had been alarmingly late, he had to catch a flight, and they only were able to give and accept the usual anxious instructions to take care of a weak pet for a couple of days. When he closed the door and left that morning, he couldn't have imagined that upon his return she would be so much more than a caretaker and healer for his dog.

But a day like today had to arrive, like the coda of a heartfelt symphony or the last page of a cherished book. Like the last morsel of cake when you are six years old and your mother allowed you two exceptional pieces because you were a loving boy. Samuel knew since the sunny moment Diana decided to stay that one unpredictable day she would open the door to inaugurate another path, followed by her music, the fake flowers that pinned the chocolate current of her hair, her bubbled laughter, and her overflowing love.

Different thoughts pounced and scrolled in Samuel's mind over the past five years. Tireless thoughts dancing in nocturnal Matisse-like rings. What had propelled the miracle? How a much younger untamable soul had chosen the house and the arms of a boringly foreseeable, mediocre paralegal and his ugly dog? How this bomb of inexplicable joy had blown up in his hands and wounded him forever? The dog would never leave, but Diana would and should.

With her few possessions and her many books his house enlightened, with her illogical conclusions his face relaxed, with her innovative rules to break the rules he and the dog gained happiness and weight. And everybody could see the change, even those who feared her and were trying to warn him about the perils of young enchantresses with deep brown eyes and penniless pockets.

Over the past five years, bliss had shaped the sporadic times when Samuel managed to forget that Diana might have been staying because of her need for shelter, because of her loneliness, because of having lost the compass of her life, because he was even lonelier and she could perceive his pleasure in taking over the rudder for the rest of their lives ... or just a while. When he could forget that her laughing may not be as sincere, or her hands as candid, or her love for the dog deeper than her love for him.

Panic and dread were more frequent visitors and poured into Samuel's ears the poison of undeniable evidence: Diana's long silences on rainy Sunday afternoons, her glimpses at elegant young men at the dog park, her obstinate refusal to talk about a past that had devoured the fine strings of her heart. Diana would retreat into secret hidden places of the mind, unattainable for Samuel, even unsolvable for the clairvoyant dog.

Thus, Samuel learned how to live and smile carrying the universal burden of knowing that the end of happiness should come and tears should be spared, that love should be accepted and let free to adopt and to be adopted, that our souls are no more than undernourished puppies, orphans wandering in a silent concealed cave where a ray of sun may enter any unexpected miraculous morning.

Samuel looked down, picked up the knife, smiled at the dog, and asked: "What's the trick to chopping onions without crying, Mutt?"

Realizations

"Just a glass of chardonnay for now, thank you," Sylvia ordered without looking up at the waiter. She had not drunk wine for lunch since last year, when in a moment of professional exhilaration, she invited herself to a sumptuous lunch at Terzo Piano, the fancy restaurant at the Art Institute. It was a blinding summer day in Chicago, and her interview for the magazine with the two curators had run smoothly, almost impeccably dictated, ready for her to transcribe it. She was sure her article would be a success and she could have it ready by midnight if her flight to LA was not delayed. At that time, looking into the crowded terrace facing Michigan Avenue, the wine had also been the reward she deserved because, at forty-five, she could still elicit lusty looks from a tweeded Renaissance expert too many lustra her elder.

But today, touched by a furtive ray of Californian sun, her wine seemed more like the prelude of the punishment she deserved for being too early to a clandestine meeting that required proper feminine tardiness. The very first rule of civilized seduction.

"Will you wait for your… friend, madam? Or you would like to order something in the meantime?"

"I will wait, thanks." Sylvia dismissed the impertinent waiter who so desperately needed a name for the relationship she still did not have with her absent lunch partner.

The illicit meeting was not a first for Sylvia. She had become attracted to the surge of adrenaline of getting to know a new gentleman once in a while the same way most of her friends had become addicted to cheap wine at 3 pm, luxurious purses that lost their fashion prevalence in three months, and beauty treatments that stretched their incipient sagging skin at the same pace as they shrunk their husbands' bank accounts. At least Sylvia's sneaky rendezvouses made her feel beautiful without stitches and sometimes, although rarely, increased the contents of her jewelry box.

Sylvia's discomfort grew with every sip. She was not familiar with this glass-walled restaurant and felt exposed and restrained. She could not turn every other minute to look at the entrance simply because her skirt was too tight and, moreover, because she did not know the features of her new fleeting lover. His pictures on the discreet affair website had been blurred and dubious. He seemed to have a handsome mane of gray hair, a muscular body, and a very well-cut blue blazer. In her silenced preliminary fantasies, he looked like a mix of Tim Roth and Liam Neeson, a dangerous devil with an angelic smile. During their brief exchange of texts, he had proved a deep knowledge of art and had even mentioned Orozco as his favorite painter. For Sylvia, the abundant gray hair and the recognition of an international artist, as superficial as it might be, were enough to initiate the choreography that led from a first secret lunch in a restaurant that none of her friends would know to the cotton-thread sheets in her favorite hotel.

Sylvia had a third filter to know if a lover was worth it: the book she used as a token to be recognized when she entered the restaurant. A book is definitely much more efficient and tactful than a red rose on a lapel. She looked at the blue book on the table and moved it away from the condensation tears of her glass. It looked like a children's book but, in reality, it was an erotic cartoon created by Aude Picault about the adventures of a lascivious countess before the French revolution. If the prospective lover expressed curiosity about the story, if he even went all the way and bought the book before meeting Sylvia, she could be sure that things would move along placidly. The affair would fit her like a cape of invisibility, like a sinful cocoon to shield her from organized family life, from mortgages and driving to karate lessons, from pot lucks and golf club bills, from bottomless discussions with the wives of her husband's colleagues about who would win the race of middle age and send their indigo children to the most expensive colleges.

"Is that you? What are you doing in this part of town? I could swear it was you when I came in. Is Cindy here too?"

Sylvia's heart somersaulted, her cheekbones tightened, and her dilated pupils got fixed on Timmy's smile.

"Hey… hi, Timmy. Eh, no, no! I'm waiting for a… an artist! I need to interview him… but he's already fifteen minutes late." Putting words together was a good strategy. The more her believable lie was knitted into sounds, the more her smile grew and the less her knees trembled. "How's everybody? I haven't seen Cindy in weeks! Thought you were all in Mayakoba for spring break."

"Oh, that… no. I got caught up with work, you know. I have this new client I was meeting today to close a deal. But he just canceled a minute ago. He said something about a medical emergency... To tell you the truth, he really sounded like he had a severe case of constipation." Timmy laughed as he mumbled the last word with one hand on the side of his face. His other hand was holding three binders full of documents.

"Tell you what. If your artist doesn't show up and my client is sick... Let's eat together. My treat! Let me take these papers back to the car. I'll be right back. Order me a glass of red, please."

By the time Sylvia's lips moved rehearsing an excuse, Timmy was crossing the parking lot, and the stiff waiter was standing at her side with his diabolic courtesy. She did not have much time. She ordered some cabernet, put away her book, and frantically fumbled through her phone until finding a new message on her private secret app: "Sorry, my lusty Countess. I cannot make it today. My wife just had a heart attack."

Sylvia did not process the tragedy of the last sentence. She had deleted the traces of her frustrated romance from all technological niches when Timmy sat across the table and smiled at her.

At 3 pm, the hour she imagined Cindy started drinking every day without Timmy fathoming such an outrage, their lunch finished. Sylvia experienced the same elation she had felt in Chicago. The same relief at something that seemed arduous and compulsory and had ended up shaking the tip of her eyelashes with laughter and ease. She was more inebriated by the innocent flirtations coming from the blonde man in front of her than from the wine. What she could not understand was Cindy's bitterness. The interminable whining about her boring relationship with Timmy that Sylvia could recite by heart. Because Timmy was not only nice and fun but he was also… quite hot.

Ten minutes later, Timmy gallantly walked her to her car and tried a very safe hug, properly maintaining his joints at the right angle and distance from hers. "Enjoy the rest of the afternoon," he said. "This was much more fun than my constipated client."

Sylvia got in the car, took off her Chloe sunglasses and put on her readers to check her phone. A message from a number she did not recognize popped up as she turned on the engine. "There's a hotel in Mayakoba that has an Orozco in the lobby. I was planning to see it with the right person. Sorry for the fake pictures. You're far sexier than the countess in your book."

Sylvia looked up. Her hand raised to her chest in the ancient gesture we all have to make one day, between our first and our last gasps for air, that unavoidable second when terror settles in the chest. And that is what Sylvia obediently did while Timmy walked away in a silent happy dance and put his phone in the side pocket of his English-cut blue blazer.

Treats

To my friend Heather Carlile with all my love,
and to Jack Waldenmaier forever.

Hannah pushed her glasses up the bridge of her nose and looked into the garden with the same intensity with which she had answered James's question once he had popped it so unexpectedly. "Would it be 'yes'? We deserve a celebration after all this love, don't you think?" During the instant that the question floated in her brain without an answer, she was able to determine that the inquiry of her beloved man was logical, poetic, and reasonably formulated. From the moment of her choked "yes" three weeks ago, the torrent of emotions and preparations had channeled methodically. Every announcement, call, and order placed in beautiful harmonic tones like the mesmerized children who had followed the vengeful piper to their end.

This morning, among the foam of her satin sheets, Hannah looked out into the garden and realized that the flowers about to come would witness a very different woman from the one who had woken up this morning in a bed too big for her. The future carer of those imminent lilies would be the absolute queen of this house whose walls were papered in music sheets, love made graciously at odd hours, and the laughter of friends after so many parties.

Hannah arose from the bed, put on a cardigan that officially belonged to James but had been repossessed by the new order of facts and, despite the cold marble beneath her feet, walked barefoot to the dining room. The garden accompanied her through the infinite windows, showering her slim figure and her long black hair with the luminescent vapors of the morning sun. Hannah observed with baffled admiration the arrangement of sweets and unnameable delicacies that Lydia, Ruth, and Phyllis, her three older cousins, and the maid, Danila, had prepared the previous day for today's reception. Every single piece of colorful candy, every coin of chocolate, seemed to have been placed by the hands of the fairies that used to guard the cribs of little princesses in old tales. And perhaps Hannah's inception as the queen of the house was the reason why she had been blessed with the magic hands of her cousins and the extra magic wand of Danila to arrange the house for today, to place all the plates and glasses in their respective piles and rows. Danila, embodying the fourth fairy who saves princesses from unjust death, had also made the cake in the shape of James's piano, following the precise instructions he had given her regarding the number of keys and pedals. He wanted all of the guests to have a morsel of sweet dough covered in the blackest chocolate as if they were able to nurture themselves with every key of his second love, the 1905 Steinway at the end of the room. Hannah did not care about cakes but these events apparently seemed incomplete without the omnipresent treat.

Hannah walked toward the piano still savoring in her nostrils the vague temptation of chocolate and praline. To compensate for the talent of the man she loved, she only knew how to play the first notes of their song. James had taught her with some sense of urgency the magic formula: C, D, A, F. She did not distinguish the notes but could always recall his fingers caressing the keyboard with the same purity with which he touched the curve of her shoulders under the stars: "In case of emergency, Dear, so you can show any lousy pianist how our song starts. You just play that and even the most unsophisticated of my friends will recognize *Our Love is Here to Stay*. And, in such an emergency, I will play it for you through their ghostly fingers if I am not around."

C, D, A, F played Hannah like invoking the spirits of all the dead composers of the world. Her eyes fell on the list of music to be played this afternoon. Hannah shuffled the pages left on the piano bench, scores that were destined for James' students, the fortunate selected to play during the reception. An eclectic deck of contemporary geniuses that James taught, played, and studied with furious passion: Stucky, Salonen, Auerbach. And also, for those who were too far away to swim from the shore of intellectual music, and for Hannah, sprinkles of delicious jazz, from Porter to Coltrane, to Ravel's compositions created after the French had fallen in love with Gershwin's arabesques.

Hannah had to hurry up. Her chorus of cousins had become disheveled medusas when she had ordered them not to come this morning to help her get dressed. "Women need help on a day like today, Darling. What you want to do is unheard of. Putting on your own makeup today? How will you make sure that all the buttons of your dress are in the right buttonhole? How will you make sure that the subtle lines of your stockings are as straight as the traces of kohl embracing your gorgeous eyes?" But Hannah had triumphed and the estrogen entourage had drowned its voices in a puddle of frustrated murmurs.

Back in her room, Hannah picked every piece of clothing from the chair, lovingly left by Danila the night before. Her dress was made of the softest silk with intricate lace decorations at the hem and the end of the sleeves. The skirt and the sleeves followed the Chanelian recommendation to fall some millimeters below knees and elbows. No decent woman over a certain age should show these betraying joints. Coco Chanel had a draconian way to define "certain age," so Hannah followed the rules out of respect and elegance. Her shoes were too bright and inconveniently high for the occasion, but she knew too well how much James loved the contour of her calves when she walked sensually in front of a crowd and this was not the day to deny any naughty moments of the past. Her last item was the tiny pill hat that had belonged to her mother. "Wear it once, Hannah," she had said, "use it for that special occasion if you happen to live it, and don't let the net cover too much of your eyes. Let people see your eyes on such a day because you will convey more through them than through words."

The bell rang apologetically. Whoever was ringing, the chauffeur most likely was being respectful of the solemn hour. Hannah had just finished cleaning the excess of her mascara. Lydia, the older fairy, had asserted that it is not the mascara itself that gets messy when you cry. "Remember what Aunty said? The problem is that women put it all over their eyelashes. Just on the tip, Darling, just on the tip, and then you tell me."

Hannah stole a piece of chocolate from the impeccable table and headed to the door. She put it in her mouth to melt while the chauffeur opened the door of the car for her. He let Hannah take her time to enter the limo as if she were a fragile onyx piece about to be shipped far away. He was an expert at discreet parsimony and revering silence during such intense moments in the life of a woman. Hannah was aware of how strange it should seem that she would go to the church without any company but, as she and James had discussed, nobody should judge decisions in matters of love that only belong to the two implicated.

Hannah took one more look at the house that would be full of guests once she returned, a new mistress of her possessions. The black leather of the limo made her feel lost, like in the belly of an oblivious whale.

Suddenly too dark, too scary. Because black seemed to be the color of this sunny day: her hair, the chocolate, the piano, the lace, the silk, the shoes, even the net almost covering her black eyelashes. The last piece of bonbon disintegrated on Hannah's tongue as her bitter revelation took shape. We do not cry when we lose our beloved because of our unused love rotting now in our hands. We cry because nobody will ever love us as the departed did. We lose the uniqueness of someone's love over us, we lose his voice, his laughter, and the cadence of his notes on the keys. Hannah's mother had been right: "Treat your love as the most precious, ephemeral treat and taste its sweetness until the end. It will hold like mascara on the tips of your soul, you will see, Darling, till the very, very end of this silly party."

Risks

She does not suspect I am this close. This cold column feels good on my cheek. From the outside, the bruise is no longer detectable. The fan of violets, purples, and pinks has faded over the past week, but the inner bruise remains with an unwinnable debate between pain and pleasure every time I press my face against a hard surface, the palm of my hand, the wood of my desk, or the granite column of this forbidden patio.

She tends not to perceive those around her. As usual, outside the class, she submerges herself into whatever story she reads. She's finished all the books from our meager classroom collection. Mrs. Malloy required everyone to bring a book from home, and all twenty-five books will sit there on the rickety shelf for the rest of the year. We should read as many as we can. At any time, Mrs. Malloy can request our reading card, where we are supposed to outline the title of the book, who wrote it, why we read it, and … if we liked it. I did want to be good this year, so I started reading the first week and then looked for the thickest book, with the most illustrations and fewest words. So far, I've read almost three books - one about a rocket that gets lost in space, one about a kid who doesn't care about school and whines all the time, and the one I am reading now, about a boy who is afraid to talk with his new schoolmates but finally finds a good soul who welcomes him. I like the stories except for the stupid rocket captain – what a coward. Did she think so too?

The book she's reading now, on the floor with her knees up and her back against a column, was given especially to her by Mrs. Malloy. From here I can see the cover: a frustrated girl with big round glasses sitting on a stool, glaring at potential readers. With her pleated skirt and a white blouse, Mary Jane shoes, and asymmetrical braids, the girl on the cover looks like the girl holding it. But the real, flesh and bone girl I see has one not two braids. A charmed snake, long and thick asleep on her shoulder.

I try to read the title of her book, but her elbow moves slightly and I retreat to the safety of my column and the shadows. From here I savor the image of her, a forbidden piece of candy during class, sweeter because nobody knows. I wonder if this is a pattern that survives growing up. But that's a hard thought, harder than any candy.

I discovered her hiding place last week after the Devereaux incident. After kicking Matthew, she ran into the corridor that only teachers, nuns, and priests are allowed to use to enter the basilica. The next morning, I followed her. She comes here every day during our long break. Always with a book and usually with some snack she brings from home. The only way into this patio is through the little door behind the altar of the smallest chapel. She must have found out that neither the gate to that chapel nor the door to the patio is ever locked. She reads and reads, leaning on the only column the sun can reach. The book on her legs, her right hand eager to turn the pages, her left hand caressing her lips. I can't get a perfect view.

I know I should talk to her. I should at least thank her. Matt Devereaux was certainly walking oddly for over a week afterward. I know why she shouted "Despereaux! You little mouse of nothing" but I want to ask her anyway. When I set my swollen cheek on my desk to take a nap during history class, I saw *The Tale of Despereaux* on the shelf. I wished she had called him a rat, but the book is about a tiny mouse, so it works in a certain way. Matt Devereaux couldn't reply after her rescue while I was lying on the tiles trying to determine whether all of my teeth were still there and my left eye was firmly in its socket. That is Devereaux's way when he talks to you and you get distracted. I'm lucky he never realized that what distracted me was her.

She turns the page as a yellow butterfly draws a ringlet of light around her head. She sees me. I am more petrified than the granite that betrays half of my body, my rumpled uniform, and one of my untied shoes.

"Uh, hi… what are you doing there?"

I cannot find my voice. It got tangled in the wing of an angel on the altar as I snuck by. I move my body from behind the column and take just one step toward her.

"Come over, there's always sun under this column in the morning. Don't you like the big patio either?"

I sit next to her on the cold tile, colder than it felt under my face on the ground after Matt Devereaux punched me. When she lowers her knees, the book falls to one side.

"How's your face? Does it still hurt? Let me see…"

She barely touches my left cheek with the tips of two fingers.

"I think you're fine," she decrees with a serious frown and smiling lips. "Look, this one is about to fall out!"

My eyes follow her fingers from my face to one of her big front teeth. She moves it slowly with dread, like caressing the tip of a cat's ear.

"My dad says that I should pull it out once and for all. What do you think?"

As she finishes her question, something compact and solid as a brick hits my neck. My whole body falls forward and my mouth collides with hers. I feel my nose pressing the side of her face and a tiny, sharp blade cuts into my lower lip. Before we can open our eyes, a cruel laughter descends.

"You idiots! I knew you were lovebirds! I'm telling Mrs. Malloy that you come here to do dirty things."

I'm only able to catch a glimpse of Matt Devereaux escaping through the door to the altar. I turn and look at her. There is blood on her chin and I am not sure if it's hers or mine. My mouth is trembling and I can taste its iron red.

This is the stupidest first kiss in history and I've ruined this page in our biography forever.

"Sorry," I mutter looking down.

"Look!" she says triumphantly. There's a tooth nestled in her hands like a baby bird. "It finally fell out."

I look at her bloody, toothless smile and I think that I have never seen one more beautiful and that I will never will. Mrs. Malloy can show me as many Mona Lisas as she wants.

"Don't …. stain your book." I stuttered.

Then she is the one leaning forward, resting her hands on my chest, kissing me for real, for the first time. She transmutes little Devereaux's last futility and cleans the blood from my lips. Of all the books that I will have read, none of them except the one I will write will have a timid spy, a mousey bully, and a toothless princess who justifies all the risks.

Directions

Victor knew he was not looking toward Algiers. The calm extension of blue in front of his window was not even the real sea and, least of all, Mediterranean waters. He was breathing the kiss between the Tagus and the Atlantic Ocean from the fourth floor of one of the oldest buildings in the oldest neighborhood of the ancient city. A soft, salty and sweet kiss between the encased waters of a river and the infinite arms of a welcoming sea. However, from this open window, caressed by a sailor breeze at this inappropriate late morning hour on a weekday, Victor's mind placed on that impossible horizon the coast of the beloved African country of his early years. He took a sip of bitter coffee, —no sugar for me, *ma belle*—, and took a second drag of the first cigarette of the day. The sting of pleasure transported him immediately to his own private lost paradise of Arabic songs and milk. Victor had a secret theory regarding memory and happiness: every adult has one lost paradise to return to available to him through mysterious smells and inarticulate sounds. The vast majority of people have been deluded by the idea that paradise is only ahead of us when, in reality, it has been already left behind and cruelly forgotten. Victor had a firm suspicion: he owed the blessing of having kept the key of his first memory to the indulgence of all the generous women he had loved or lusted for in his quite long life. Magical women like the one who had materialized in his life two days ago and had disturbed his apollonian peace like the earthquake that had gutted this city more than two centuries ago.

Annette came from the tiny bathroom, drying her hair with a towel. She wore a white sundress too loose for her waist and too revealing for her inviting breasts that reminded him of cane sugar and caramel syrup. She sat on the smaller couch shaking a bottle of lotion. She put one leg on the coffee table pretending she was not aware that he was looking and started examining her crimson toenails with the delicacy of an entomologist.

"Are you alright, *chéri*?" she asked without looking up. "You seem so pensive there. I guess you are not talkative in the morning. I need to remember that."

She did not wait for an answer, opened the bottle, and poured some lotion on her knee. At fifty Victor had already learned a priceless lesson, not all feminine questions are uttered for an answer. For some incomprehensible reason, defiant to the masculine logic, most of his lovers and official girlfriends had used the interrogative tone frequently to make assertive comments or to express a feeling. Men should be aware, Victor reminded himself, that the question of a woman is like a carrier pigeon whose most important message is the one it brings, not the one it carries back. Victor perceived that Annette was not asking him about his thoughts so he would tell her. She wanted to let him know that she cared about his meditations as much as she had cared to learn how much sugar he wanted in his coffee. Victor did not answer. She continued applying lotion on her leg with the same determination with which she had planned this unfathomable trip to this conjuring city after so many years, after so much silence and so very few romantic encounters in their past. She did not look around for hints, she did not wait for suggestions.

Victor went back to his coffee and the view and enveloped himself one more time in the smell of the waves. He was certain that the house of his childhood in Algiers was not close to the coast, but the smell of the sea was part of Zahli's smell. His *fatma*, his nanny, smelled like seaweed and iron, like rounded stones left in the sun for too long, like milk and salt. Victor felt the soothing whisper of his most innocent secret, the memory he had not shared even once in his life. Unlike so many people who would hunt for happiness in front of them, Victor was aware that his moment of supreme completion had happened already and he was thankful that he had been able to capture it and label it as the starting point of his conscious life: being not even three, lost in the magnanimous breasts of Zahli, amorously fed by her even when *Maman* was not happy with the disobedient idea.

Annette finished with her left leg and raised the right one to the table slowly caressing those hidden corners of her knees that he had kissed desperately not even an hour ago. Inclined as she was over her thighs, Victor could see the lace ruffle of her dress above her chest. Exactly like the brim of Zahli's *niqāb*, that he used to touch with the tip of impossibly small fingers trying to unveil the notes of her monotonous songs, while he received her motherly milk with regal pleasure. The anecdote in the house, the memory he could not possibly have, was that *Maman* had discovered Zahli's act of rebellion after her second day of voluntary work at the French embassy. Practical and organized, the young worldly mother of two, with a feminist revolutionary heart, was trying to cope with the new reality that her family would live in the former colony for some years, that her husband had received an immense professional opportunity, and that she had to accept the challenge of raising two little boys in a foreign country with the help of a woman who barely spoke her language.

Annette tripped the bottle of lotion with her foot but was fast enough to catch it before its silky content touched the doubtfully clean carpet of the vacation flat. Victor heard her movements but continued looking through the window, smoking, recreating in his mind the unwitnessed moment when *Maman* had opened the refrigerator for the second day in a row and had found untouched the four bottles she had left in the morning for the baby. Manually pumping four bottles of milk was not an easy task in the late sixties, seeing them still full and unusable at the end of the day was even more painful. But the image of baby Victor sleeping so soundly, cooed by the Arabic notes of his *fatma*, who was at the same time breastfeeding the youngest of her own three boys, made *Maman* know the answer to her complaint before being able to structure it in a French that was comprehensible enough for Zahli: milk in a bottle was not good enough for any baby in the care of a responsible *fatma* with breasts as generous as her incommensurable love.

Annette looked up again and this time freed a question that did require an answer. "What are you thinking of, *chéri*? You have that strange smile. Are you thinking about me, about us, about how crazy I am, about how magical all this is?" Her eyes were again on her toes when she finished the question, but the direction of her body let him know she was ready for a new dangerous hug. A hug that might push even later their planned excursion to the beach.

Victor turned to her taking a last drag from his cigarette, put it out on the sill, and threw the brown dead butt through the window with a movement too many times rehearsed. He looked deeply into Annette's black eyes and then down into the welcoming lace ruffle on her chest. Before the words came to his mouth, his brain produced an atom of light that included, like the magic Aleph, the past, present and future of a mature man who sometimes felt lost and alone for too long and knew he had to stop smoking forever.

"I was just recalling my very first memory."

"What is it? I bet it is about some beautiful girl you fell in love with when you were three. I can see you, handsome little brat breaking the hearts of female infants!" Annette said with a sarcastic smile.

"Well, it is not exactly like that. But it has to do with a foreign woman like you and her breasts."

"See? After all these years without any contact and I can see through you like you through that window!"

"Do you know what a *fatma* is?"

And for the first time, Victor told a woman, this very woman who tasted like cane sugar and caramel, the only memory that he had kept hidden all his life. Drowning in the well of her eyes and the waves of her dress, Victor discovered that it was still possible to turn the compass of lost paradise at ease into a new path, into a new perfect direction.

Sounds

The second time Roger was hurt by the shriek of the brakes he raised his deformed hand and turned off the volume of the hearing aid. He still had twenty minutes of solitude and was not going to waste them bearing the poking noises around him: doors opening every other block, the worthless conversation of the passenger sitting next to him discussing irrelevant scores that would be forgotten in hours, the blasting hideous music that came out of the headphones of a young, beefy woman on the other side of the bus. He still had some time. How different this excursion could have been if he had still been allowed to drive. He would have been cocooned by the quietude of his old Mercedes, by its sheltering silence only punctuated by the low echo of Mahler's piano concerto. But the last years had been an interminable lost battle to retain permission, to preserve his freedom. He had lost every bastion at a fast pace: living in his own cluttered house, cooking his own food, driving to wherever the fuck he wanted, even meeting with his few friends to play poker. The truth was that the last option had been dictated more by death than by the growing authority of Allyssa. His friends had died faster than his daughter's ability to ban them from his life because they were not good influences for him anymore.

Roger looked through the window and dreaded one more time his task for the afternoon. He was elated that for some hours he could leave that horror house of old specters and still be able to do it on his own, but it was a task nevertheless. To spend four hours with a five-year-old, to eat some crappy children's food, and endure an imbecile kid play was not his most ideal plan. On the other hand, because he could not read much before his eyes turned foggy and a symphony didn't sound the same through his hearing device, he decided to accept this impromptu date with his great-grandchild. Roger had not seen the boy in a long time. Tina, his only granddaughter, was too busy being an adult and raising a child. She barely came to the house of horrors, and he could not blame her for that. If only Allyssa, her mother, had less time to come and organize his life and stipulate the new rules of his disguised imprisonment.

Giving up driving had been the worst, even worse than abandoning the house. You can always leave a house you hate as long as you have the means to move away from it. He had exercised that trick during the middle stages of this marriage. He had hated the home more than the house, truly, but had been able to pass through those shadowy years of discontent with the delicate excuses of work and other manly responsibilities. Then life moved on, Alyssa left the house, their granddaughter was born and the peace of retirement descended upon him and his wife covering them with a hefty layer of silent snowflakes that kept them civilized and even friendly until he was entitled a widower.

The bus stopped again. This time in front of a big billboard with a long-lined, big-breasted volleyball player in a red bikini. Roger's eyes followed her figure while tracing the realization that his life had been dictated mostly by the immovable will of women. His taciturn wife, a short-time mistress who had died too young, his charging daughter full of solutions, and the rebellious granddaughter who had dared to conceive a child without any known father because, according to the new protocol, men were not necessary enough.

Roger smiled. God had taken revenge. He had sent Tina a boy. "Deal with that, superwoman. I hope your son is necessary enough," Roger muttered just to savor the inaudible words. He turned his blurry eyes up to the sky through the bus window and gave the clouds a thump-up with his right hand, his good hand, whose fingers hurt him less. His left hand's contorted claws had been the ultimate reason for those idiots not renewing his driving license. He had not shared the pain with anybody, only God and he knew how much those scrawny bones really hurt.

Roger couldn't see properly when the bus braked at his designated stop. He guessed that Tina and the little boy were there waiting for him. He turned up the volume of his hearing device to welcome the explosion of the opening doors. His granddaughter looked older, tired, and eager to leave her skinny child in his hands to run to whatever commitment she had this Sunday afternoon.

"Hi, Pappo," she said while blowing a fake kiss on his right cheek. "You look fantastic! Here is Maddox who is very excited to spend time with you. Aren't you, darling? Do you remember Pappo?"

Maddox looked up at Roger and frowned his nose with doubt, curiosity, and amazement, in the guiltless way that only the very young or the very old can master. "Here are the tickets for the show. You have to walk two blocks to the Dancing Crocodile. Maddox likes his burger without cheese and the small green ice cream with crocodile marshmallow teeth in it. Don't you darling? Pappo, make sure that he gets only the small ice cream, OK? The show starts at 4:30 and it's just around the corner from the restaurant. You both will have a great time. It's Jack and the Beanstalk, a real classic! I'll meet you at the theater's door at 6:45. Any questions? Are you going to have fun?"

Roger felt an immediate compassion for the serious boy with a ridiculous name. It wouldn't be easy for him to deal with a mother who pretended to be so orderly and zappy. Both males shook and nodded their heads consecutively, more to please Tina than to show that her message was received. She ran away and got in a cab without looking back or waving either to the oldest or the youngest love of her life.

Once his mother was surely gone, Maddox looked up and uttered a few words that Roger did not understand.

"You need to speak louder, young man. I am an old guy. Do you see this thing in my ear? I am a little deaf. If we are going to have some valuable exchange of words today, you have to speak up."

Maddox sighed and repeated almost yelling: "Can I have a big ice cream… sir?"

Roger put his eyebrows together in the exact same way his great-grandson, 82 years his junior, had done it minutes before and looked at him with mute pride and bewilderment.

"Of course, you can. Do you think we are going to obey that blabby mother of yours? Neither of us is of age to behave. You can have the biggest ice cream ever and dip it in chocolate and cover it with sprinkles and M&Ms if you like."

It took Maddox three seconds of deep meditation to process the verdict.

"Hurry up, Pappo," he yelled one more time.

Then, taking the first step, little Maddox clutched Roger's hand with much strength and determination. He would never remember that it was Roger's left hand he grabbed to guide him promptly. He would never have a way to know how the brutal pain resonated in his great-grandfather's brain. Fortunately for both of them, the harmonic wave of love echoed in Roger's heart much faster, much truer, and first.

Conquered by Fog

The problem was not that they did not know. The problem was that when they got to know, when the only enlightened one had come back to unveil the truth for them, they had chosen to remain inside the cave, mesmerized by the shadows, engulfed by darkness. As if they had chosen not to see. What people choose not to believe is usually more interesting and ironic than whatever fantasy they decide to follow for life. Rita had always interpreted the drama of Plato's allegory that way. And she wondered often what strange switch makes souls turn into the rocky surface instead of accepting the blinding truth of the sun. To her, it was the allegory of choosing a lie even when confronted with clear evidence, the most voluntary and tenacious form of belief. The acceptance of the unreal, dancing shadows coming off the wall because the fear of the real light might show our own disgusting insignificance. She could still see the look of offended pride from Professor Lauret when she dared to express the thought, followed by some looks of disdain and boredom from her classmates in Introduction to Philosophy. As a freshman taking one of those proemial classes that a pompous hunger for intellectuality had pushed her to attend, Rita had defied her professor, who had reacted in a belligerent manner probably more out of tiredness than defeat.

"Mrs. Thielemann, the doctor is ready. Second room to your right, please."

Rita came back from the safety of the images that had triggered the memory of her early years untangling Plato´s allegories of caves and fires. All those posters of dog eyes, the naked anatomy wisely hidden under the furry lids, those cavernous pupils, open wells of black depth surrounded by caramel irises. Magic lanterns of wonder and love. Piper's pupils had long ago stopped being such mirrors of the night. Nowadays, her eyes seem more like the highest caves that Rita had seen in Granada, in the Gardens of Sacromonte, the ones far up in the hills where the gypsies lived, curtained by clouds to veil the entrance of their abode made of rock and stalagmites. Milky and hollow were the eyes of Rita's dog today, the happy eyes about to get a verdict from Dr. Douglas in Lexington, the eminence in veterinarian ophthalmology. Seven miles from home to hear the death sentence of a Labrador's sight, Piper's panting started accelerating, echoing the anxiety of the animal and the dread of a woman's heart.

"Mrs. Thielemann, Piper?" Dr. Douglas petted Piper's left ear, the one that always looked a little tired, crooked. "Very nice to meet you. We have some news…"

"Hello…" Rita put her purse on a low chair and looked up at the doctor with straightened lips that wanted to mock a smile. "So…"

"Well, as Dr. Reed suspected…, and she was right to refer you to our office, Piper has become totally blind. She may have been this way for the last four to six months."

Rita squeezed Piper's blue leash as if the pressure of her hand on the leather could restrain

-

imminent sobs. "Totally? Not even shadows? Is there anything she can see? I swear she…"

"Yes, I know." Dr. Douglas said very matter-of-factly while Rita frowned. "We hear that all the time. She is not stumbling upon things, she knows where everything is. But animals are very good at hiding their losses, at compensating, you know. Much better than humans, to tell you the truth."

Rita did not like the pedagogic tone. She felt the same pang of disgust that Professor Lauret had seeded so many years ago.

"Will she be okay? How can I help her? Do we need to prepare the house in a certain way?"

"There is nothing you can do. First, because you didn't when you didn't know and Piper was fine. Second, because dogs see with their noses more than with their eyes. Smells are her colors. For her, every object, every being, is the added smells provoked by every one of its atoms."

"I am not sure I follow you."

"For her, you are the smell of your hair, the sweat of your hands, the scent of grass in the hem of your skirt. She can also smell your emotions. She can see you and me, much deeper than with her eyes. She will be fine, Mrs. Thielemann. But remember, she can also sense your sorrow. Just give her two extra treats every day in memory of her beautiful eyes conquered by fog."

Driving back to Concord, grabbing the wheel with the same desperation as she had held her dog's leash, Rita wondered if Piper could smell the tears falling on her green skirt. And against all her platonic rules, Rita chose to believe that everything was as it has always been, that her old dog was not blind and that she would never die. Piper kept snoring in the back seat, her left ear canopying over one dead caramel eye.

I would like to express my deepest gratitude to four generous souls without whom this book would not have been possible.

To Ian Perrex, for your support, wisdom, and time. Your observations dress my words in a magic literary cloak.

To Quin Mathews, to whom this book is dedicated. Thanks for your patience, your effervescent encouragement, and all your teachings. Thank you for the exquisite picture on the cover of this book.

To Pierre Turcotte, for this new opportunity.

To Robert, for everything.

Except for "Risks," all of the stories in this book have been published in literary magazines and journals. At the time of this publication the short story "Conquered by Fog" is nominated for the 2023 Pushcart Prize.

Here is a list of those publications:

"Thief", Ponder Review, Vol. 4, Issue 2, The Mississippi University for Women, 2020, p. 35.

"Stupidity", The Closed Eye Open, Issue II, 2020.

"Sounds", The Halcyone, Vol. 3, Number 3, 2021. p. 23.

"Directions", Mediterranean Poetry, 2021.

"Realizations", Libretto Magazine (Nigeria), Issue 5, 2021.

"Kicks", Heartland Society of Women Writers, 2021.

"Treats", Egophobia Journal (Romania), 2021.

"Hidden Places", Manawaker Flash Fiction Podcast, 2021.

"Truth", Manawaker Flash Fiction Podcast, 2022.

"Conquered by Fog", Freshwater Literary Journal, Asnuntuck Community College, 2022, p. 91.

"Predictions", Crossing the Tees Firth Short Story Anthology, Middlesbrough, Crossing the Tees, 2002, p. 172.

ABOUT THE AUTHOR

Fabiana Elisa Martínez was born in Buenos Aires, Argentina, where she graduated from the Universidad Católica Argentina with a degree in Linguistics and World Literature. She is a linguist, a language teacher, and a writer. She speaks English, Spanish, French, Portuguese, and Italian. She has lived in Dallas, Texas, for more than twenty years. She is the author of the short story collection *12 Random Words*, her first work of fiction and recipient of ten international awards; the podcast and grammar book *Spanish 360 with Fabiana*; and the short story *Stupidity*, published in electronic format as an independent book by Pierre Turcotte Editor. Other short stories of hers have been published over five continents in *Rigorous Magazine*, *The Closed Eye Open*, *Ponder Review*, *Hindsight Magazine*, *The Good Life Review* (UK), *The Halcyone*, *Rhodora Magazine* (India), *Mediterranean Poetry*, *Writers and Readers Magazine* (UK), *Libretto Magazine* (Nigeria), *Automatic Pilot* (Ireland), *Lusitania* (Buenos Aires), *The Pilgrims of the Plate* (Buenos Aires), *Heartland Society of Women Writers*, *Egophobia Journal* (Romania), *Defunkt Magazine*, *Brilliant Flash Fiction*, *Freshwater Literary Journal*, *Syncopation Literary Journal*, *The Raven's Perch*, *Write Now Literary Journal*, *Defuncted Journal*; and the anthologies *Writers of Tomorrow*, *Pure Slush-Love, Lifespan 4 Anthology* (Australia), the *2022 Wordrunner Anthology*, the *Crossing the Tees Firth Short Story Anthology* (UK), and *Pure Slush-Marriage, Lifespan 6 Anthology* (Australia). Two short stories were broadcast as part of the Manawaker Flash Fiction Podcast.

FROM THE SAME AUTHOR

LANGUAGES

SPANISH 360 WITH FABIANA – VOLUME I (2020)
SPANISH 360 WITH FABIANA – VOLUME II (2020)

SHORT STORIES

12 RANDOM WORDS – 12 PALABRAS AL AZAR (2016)
12 RANDOM WORDS – 12 MOTS AU HASARD (2017)
12 RANDOM WORDS – 12 PALAVRAS AO ACASO
    (2018)
STUPIDITY, *Pierre Turcotte Editor* (2021)
CONQUERED BY FOG, *Pierre Turcotte Editor* (2023)

TABLE OF CONTENTS

Cover image: "Untitled" by Quin Mathews.
Photo of the author : Kris Hundt.

Pierre Turcotte Éditeur
10393, avenue Christophe-Colomb
Montréal (Québec) H2C 2V1
Canada

turcotte.pierre@gmail.com

https://en.pierreturcotte.com

Made in the USA
Columbia, SC
15 July 2023

20070802R00078